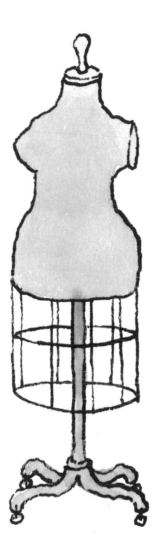

Brave Irene

by William Steig

A Sunburst Book
Farrar, Straus and Giroux

For Jeanne

Mrs. Bobbin, the dressmaker, was tired and had a bad headache, but she still managed to sew the last stitches in the gown she was making.

"It's the most beautiful dress in the whole world!" said her daughter, Irene. "The duchess will love it."

"It *is* nice," her mother admitted. "But, dumpling, it's for tonight's ball, and I don't have the strength to bring it. I feel sick."

"Poor Mama," said Irene. "I can get it there!"

"No, cupcake, I can't let you," said Mrs. Bobbin. "Such a huge package, and it's such a long way to the palace. Besides, it's starting to snow."

"But I *love* snow," Irene insisted. She coaxed her mother into bed, covered her with two quilts, and added a blanket for her feet. Then she fixed her some tea with lemon and honey and put more wood in the stove.

With great care, Irene took the splendid gown down from the dummy and packed it in a big box with plenty of tissue paper.

"Dress warmly, pudding," her mother called in a weak voice, "and don't forget to button up. It's cold out there, and windy."

Irene put on her fleece-lined boots, her red hat and muffler, her heavy coat, and her mittens. She kissed her mother's hot forehead six times, then once again, made sure she was tucked in snugly, and slipped out with the big box, shutting the door firmly behind her.

It really was cold outside, very cold. The wind whirled the falling snow-flakes about, this way, that way, and into Irene's squinting face. She set out on the uphill path to Farmer Bennett's sheep pasture.

By the time she got there, the snow was up to her ankles and the wind was worse. It hurried her along and made her stumble. Irene resented this; the box was problem enough. "Easy does it!" she cautioned the wind, leaning back hard against it.

By the middle of the pasture, the flakes were falling thicker. Now the wind drove Irene along so rudely she had to hop, skip, and go helter-skeltering over the knobby ground. Cold snow sifted into her boots and chilled her feet. She pushed out her lip and hurried on. This was an important errand.

When she reached Apple Road, the wind decided to put on a show.
It ripped branches from trees and flung them about, swept up and
scattered the fallen snow, got in front of Irene to keep her from moving
ahead. Irene turned around and pressed on backwards.

"Go home!" the wind squalled. "Irene . . . go hooooooome . . ."

"I will do no such thing," she snapped. "No such thing, you wicked wind!"

"Go ho—o—ome," the wind yodeled. "GO HO—WO—WOME," it shrieked, "or else." For a short second, Irene wondered if she shouldn't heed the wind's warning. But no! *The gown had to get to the duchess!*

The wind wrestled her for the package—walloped it, twisted it, shook it, snatched at it. But Irene wouldn't yield. "It's my mother's work!" she screamed.

Then—oh, woe!—the box was wrenched from her mittened grasp and sent bumbling along in the snow. Irene went after it.

She pounced and took hold, but the ill-tempered wind ripped the box open. The ball gown flounced out and went waltzing through the powdered air with tissue-paper attendants.

Irene clung to the empty box and watched the beautiful gown disappear.

How could anything so terribly wrong be allowed to happen? Tears froze on her lashes. Her dear mother's hard work, all those days of measuring, cutting, pinning, stitching . . . for *this*? And the poor duchess! Irene decided she would have to trudge on with just the box and explain everything in person.

She went shuffling through the snow. Would her mother understand, she wondered, that it was the wind's fault, not hers? Would the duchess be angry? The wind was howling like a wild animal.

Suddenly Irene stepped in a hole and fell over with a twisted ankle. She blamed it on the wind. "Keep quiet!" she scolded. "You've done enough damage already. You've spoiled everything! *Everything!*" The wind swallowed up her words.

She sat in the snow in great pain, afraid she wouldn't be able to go on. But she managed to get to her feet and start moving. It hurt. Home, where she longed to be, where she and her mother could be warm together, was far behind. It's got to be closer to the palace, she thought. But where any place was in all this snow, she couldn't be sure.

She plowed on, dragging furrows with her sore foot. The short winter day was almost done.

Am I still going the right way, she wondered. There was no one around to advise her. Whoever else there was in this snow-covered world was far, far away, and safe indoors—even the animals in their burrows. She went plodding on.

Soon night took over. She knew in the dark that the muffled snow was still falling—she could feel it. She was cold and alone in the middle of nowhere. Irene was lost.

She had to keep moving. She was hoping she'd come to a house, any house at all, and be taken in. She badly needed to be in someone's arms. The snow was above her knees now. She shoved her way through it, clutching the empty box.

She was asking how long a small person could keep this struggle up, when she realized it was getting lighter. There was a soft glow coming from somewhere below her.

She waded toward this glow, and soon was gazing down a long slope at a brightly lit mansion. It had to be the palace!

Irene pushed forward with all her strength and—*sloosh! thwump!*—
she plunged downward and was buried. She had fallen off a little cliff.
Only her hat and the box in her hands stuck out above the snow.

Even if she could call for help, no one would hear her. Her body shook.
Her teeth chattered. Why not freeze to death, she thought, and let all
these troubles end. Why not? She was already buried.

And never see her mother's face again? Her good mother who smelled like fresh-baked bread? In an explosion of fury, she flung her body about to free herself and was finally able to climb up on her knees and look around.

How to get down to that glittering palace? As soon as she raised the question, she had the answer.

She laid the box down and climbed aboard. But it pressed into the snow and stuck. She tried again, and this time, instead of climbing on, she leaped. The box shot forward, like a sled.

The wind raced after Irene but couldn't keep up. In a moment she would be with people again, inside where it was warm. The sled slowed and jerked to a stop on paving stones.

The time had come to break the bad news to the duchess. With the empty box clasped to her chest, Irene strode nervously toward the palace.

But then her feet stopped moving and her mouth fell open. She stared. Maybe this was impossible, yet there it was, a little way off and over to the right, hugging the trunk of a tree—the beautiful ball gown! The wind was holding it there.

"Mama!" Irene shouted. "Mama, I found it!"

  She managed somehow, despite the wind's meddling, to get the gown off the tree and back in its box. And in another moment she was at the door of the palace. She knocked twice with the big brass knocker. The door opened and she burst in.

She was welcomed by cheering servants and a delirious duchess. They couldn't believe she had come over the mountain in such a storm, all by herself. She had to tell the whole story, every detail. And she did.

Then she asked to be taken right back to her sick mother. But it was out of the question, they said; the road that ran around the mountain wouldn't be cleared till morning.

"Don't fret, child," said the duchess. "Your mother is surely sleeping now. We'll get you there first thing tomorrow."

Irene was given a good dinner as she sat by the fire, the moisture steaming off her clothes. The duchess, meanwhile, got into her freshly ironed gown before the guests began arriving in their sleighs.

What a wonderful ball it was! The duchess in her new gown was like
a bright star in the sky. Irene in her ordinary dress was radiant. She was

swept up into dances by handsome aristocrats, who kept her feet off the
floor to spare her ankle. Her mother would enjoy hearing all about it.

Early the next morning, when snow had long since ceased falling,
Mrs. Bobbin woke from a good night's sleep feeling much improved. She
hurried about and got a fire going in the cold stove. Then she went to look
in on Irene.

But Irene's bed was empty! She ran to the window and gazed at the
white landscape. No one out there. Snow powder fell from the branch of
a tree.

"Where is my child?" Mrs. Bobbin cried. She whipped on her coat to go out and find her.

When she pulled the door open, a wall of drift faced her. But peering over it, she could see a horse-drawn sleigh hastening up the path. And seated on the sleigh, between two large footmen, was Irene herself, asleep but smiling.

Would you like to hear the rest?

Well, there was a bearded doctor in the back of the sleigh. And the duchess had sent Irene's mother a ginger cake with white icing, some oranges and a pineapple, and spice candy of many flavors, along with a note saying how much she cherished her gown, and what a brave and loving person Irene was.

Which, of course, Mrs. Bobbin knew. Better than the duchess.